REAPER

A HORROR NOVELLA

JONATHAN PONGRATZ

Reaper: A Horror Novella by Jonathan Pongratz

Cover by Mario Lampic.

ABOUT REAPER

Gregory and his little sister Imogen love spending Halloween with their parents. But this year is different. If he proves he can take care of Imogen all by himself, he'll finally have the allowance he's dreamed of.

That was before the basement door opened on its own. Before the strange door appeared in the basement and Imogen was taken from him by the monster.

Now everyone in town is blaming him for her disappearance, but no one is listening to his story. Where did the door come from? What was that creature? And most of all, can he find his sister before it's too late, or will he bury his memories of her along with his parents?

I would like to dedicate this story to my mother, who never gave up on me and my dreams.

PREFACE

The boogeyman doesn't exist. That's what your parents tell you, what they're supposed to tell you. But now I know better. If you're reading this now, it may already be too late. I don't know how far this thing goes, or if there's even a way out of all this. I don't expect you to take my word for it, but maybe, just maybe if you pay attention, you won't make the same mistake that I did. Maybe you can get out before they come for you too.

CHAPTER 1

"Gregory, Imogen! We're leaving!" Mom called from downstairs.

I raced down with my seven-year old sister, jumping over the last step to beat her to the ground floor.

"I win!" I teased with a ruffling of her brown curly hair. She slapped my hand away and grimaced before crossing her arms.

Mom smiled at us as she fastened a pearl earring to her ear and smoothed her fancy black dress. She snatched a pumpkin bowl off the counter and lowered it to me. "You're on candy duty tonight, sweetie. Are you sure you can handle this?"

I grinned from ear to ear and nodded. After begging and pleading for the past two years, my parents had finally decided I was ready to watch over my little sister without a babysitter. If I proved myself tonight, I wouldn't have to deal with our smelly neighbor Erica and her early bedtimes anymore. Even better, I'd finally have an allowance.

I looked into the plastic pumpkin in my hands. Reese's, Hersheys, Gobstoppers, the works. None of that nasty coconut crap. My stomach gurgled.

I glanced up at my mom and plugged my nose. "Where are the stinky candles?" Every year, she lit up a ton of these odd-smelling candles. I had gotten used to the odor, but it was strange that the whole house wasn't littered with them already.

Mom looked shocked for a moment, then she smiled sweetly. "Oh, we don't need those this year. Are you sure you're ready for tonight? I can always call Erica." She reached for the phone.

"No, no!" I shouted, swiping it from her. "Everything will be just fine. Me and Immy will watch tv and answer the door. It'll be easy. Come on Mom, I'm thirteen. I can do this."

"That's my big little man." Mom's gaze focused on me, and for a moment she almost looked sad before she turned and walked into the kitchen, her heels clicking on the tile. "George! It's time to go!"

In a fleeting moment my parents were gone, leaving me and my little sister behind. I lingered in the foyer, my mind swimming with fantasies of the things I'd be able to buy once I had an allowance.

"I wanna go trick-or-treating," Imogen whined from behind me.

I spun around and rolled my eyes. Was she going to be like this all night? "We can't. Mom and Dad need us to stay here."

"But I wanna play dress up!" Imogen stomped her feet, tears rolling down her face.

Crap, here we go. I reached into the bucket and waved my sister's favorite candy in front of her until she stopped crying. The last thing I needed was a night of neverending hissy fits and screaming. She grabbed for the Snickers bar, but I pulled it just out of her reach.

"Look, we're not supposed to eat any of this candy, but if you promise to stay calm and help me with the trick-or-treaters, you can have this."

Imogen sniffled and wiped at her eyes. "Two?"

I shrugged. "Maybe. Depends how much you help me."

My little sister snatched the candy out of my hand and raced towards the living room in a fit of giggles.

I dragged my feet after her. *Here we go.*

———

THE NEXT HOUR or so went by a lot smoother. Imogen ate her candy and was happy to run around the house. I turned on the tv in the living room for some scary movie time and heated up some popcorn. We'd only had a few knocks on the door, and throwing candy at whoever showed up was easy enough.

It had to have been twenty minutes since the last trick or treater came by, and I was almost tempted to turn the front porch lights off just to enjoy the rest of my night. But the promise of wealth, comic books, and video games echoed through my head. I sighed and jammed another fistful of popcorn into my mouth.

At least *Under the Bed* was on. It wasn't my favorite scary movie anymore, but the jump scares and otherworldly monsters were so realistic it used to give me nightmares.

On the screen, a reptilian monster with grey scaly skin and razor-sharp teeth was emerging from under a little girl's bed. The floorboards under the monster creaked, and the blonde girl shifted in her sleep but didn't wake up. The monster paused, but slowly crept towards her, stretching his mouth open as he got closer until it was wide enough to attempt to eat her. The monster drooled hungrily.

Imogen suddenly screamed at the top of her lungs behind the couch. I jumped, spilling popcorn everywhere and fumbling off the sofa.

"What the heck is your problem?" I shouted, scrambling to my feet.

"S-scary!" she sobbed back.

Dang it. I grabbed the remote and changed the channel, skipping some cheesy episode of Full House, then another with the words 'Have You Seen Me?' featuring a sad kid's face below. I settled on some weird show with two giant bananas dancing around in their pajamas. Imogen planted herself on the floor in front of me and continued to cry.

"Hey, see that?" I said, pointing to the screen. "Isn't that funny? Bananas can't dance." My sister wailed in response.

I quickly reached into the candy bucket and drew out another Snickers bar. She snatched it greedily and went to town, leaving chocolate smears all around her mouth. *Ugh, disgusting.*

I went into the kitchen and grabbed a paper towel. Imogen grumbled as I wiped around her mouth. "You're a mess." After I finished cleaning her up, she jumped to her feet, clearly over her scary encounter.

"Hide and seek," she stated.

"Immy, no. I have to pass out candy to the trick-or-treaters or Mom and Dad will whoop me."

"Hide. And. Seek," she said, this time with her eyebrows furrowed.

I started to protest again when the doorbell rang. I scooped up the candy bucket from the couch and headed to the door. "We'll talk about this in a minute."

I opened the door and was greeted by a witch, a werewolf, and another kid covered in a white sheet with two holes cut out for eyes. I grinned. *How original.*

After I tossed some candy into the kids' bags and shooed them away, I shut the door and headed back to the living room.

"Alright Immy, if you promise to be good I--" I stopped. Where was she? The house was eerily quiet. I search the living room, but she wasn't there. "This isn't funny!" I yelled.

I was going to tell her we could play until the next trick or treater knocked, but now I was just pissed.

"Come back to the living room!" I commanded, doing my best impersonation of Dad's stern tone. No response. I plopped the candy bucket on the couch and stomped out of the living room, determined to find my little brat sister. If I missed a single trick-or-treater I was going to kill her.

I checked the dining room, kitchen, and laundry room on the ground floor, not missing a single hiding spot I used to squish into, but there was no sign of my little sister. Where the hell was she? Imogen was shorter and thinner than I was at her age. Could she have found a hiding spot I hadn't thought of? *Dang it.*

I wandered around in a baffled shuffle, a shiver running down my spine as I passed by the basement door at the foot of the staircase. Imogen and I both shared a fear of our dark cavern of a basement. Mom and Dad kept it locked, but the few times we'd been down there it was frigid and eerie, like something was waiting with little icy fingers to grab at you.

I passed the basement and ended up at the foot of the staircase, glancing up. All of our bedrooms were upstairs, and there were a couple of closets and bathrooms up there too. *That's where she is*, I told myself.

I started with my bedroom since I knew it like the back of my hand. I checked under my bed, behind the curtains, in my closet and old toy chest. But Immy wasn't in there. I groaned and got up to my feet. *Where the hell is she?* Suddenly, I heard a loud thud somewhere nearby and ran out of my room. I listened for the noise again. *Knock, knock, knock.*

The door! I bolted down the stairs, snatching the candy bucket on my way without stopping. I yanked the door open to see the backside of a fairy, a stormtrooper, and a kid in a suit with a mask on.

"Hey, don't go!" I panted.

The kids jumped. They turned around and stared at me like I was out of my mind.

"No, seriously, have some candy," I said, presenting the pumpkin-shaped bucket. They took their fair share of candy hesitantly, and I closed the door with a sigh, closing my eyes. *That was close.*

When I opened my eyes again, Imogen was at the base of the stairs. She had a doe-eyed expression on her face like a deer in headlights.

"You!" I roared.

She ran towards the laundry room and I darted after her.

"This is all your fault!" I screamed, chasing her into the adjoining kitchen. "Why can't you just do what you're told?"

Imogen sprinted through our kitchen to the dining room and expertly ducked under the table to the other side. I mimicked her actions, but underestimated my height and smacked my head on the edge of the table.

I cried out as I fell on my back and put my hands to my forehead. My head throbbed in short, sharp bursts. There would definitely be an ugly bruise tomorrow. "Ugh, Immy!"

My little sister scampered away while I cringed on the floor.

Knock, knock, knock.

"Not now!" I bellowed.

Knock, knock, knock.

"Just hold on a minute!" Grumbling in protest, I jumped to my feet, but my balance was way off. I swayed into the chair next to me, knocking it down and falling with it to the ground again. "Damn it!"

Knock, knock, knock.

This time I got up to my feet as slowly as I dared. I still wobbled a little, and my head pulsated, but I didn't fall. It felt like an eternity before I got to the front door with the candy bucket in hand. I opened the door. No one was there. I poked my head outside.

Numerous groups of kids walked down the street. It

could've been any of them. My heart sank; it was too late. A sudden anger came over me, and I slammed the door shut as heat flushed to my face.

I threw the candy bucket at the ground, treats spilling out everywhere. Who even cared about this Halloween crap anyways? Mom and Dad weren't here, so how would they know I missed a group of trick-or-treaters? Besides, this was my little sister's fault, not mine.

The loud creaking of a door interrupted my angry thoughts. Next to the base of the stairs, the basement door slowly screeched open, the long padlock on it hanging open on the latch. A cold tingle ran down my back. How was the door open? Could Imogen have found the key? No, no, no. It was impossible.

I walked up to the open door reluctantly. There was no key in the lock. I peered into the black darkness, my heart racing. "Immy?" I called. No response. I reached into the darkness for the light switch and flipped it on, but nothing happened.

I moaned in frustration. What possessed my sister to go down in the basement with no light? Was she out of her freaking mind? She probably wanted to get back at me for getting mad at her. I was almost tempted to close the door on her, but that would be cruel. That and if Mom and Dad caught her down there they'd freak.

I dragged myself to the kitchen and snatched the flashlight under the sink before heading back to the basement door and clicking it on. *Great, just great.*

CHAPTER 2

I shined my flashlight on the wooden steps leading below, doing my best to stay calm as a frigid chill raised goosebumps on my arms and legs. *There's nothing down here but your stupid little sister. Monsters don't exist. You're being a baby.*

Ignoring my own thoughts, I forced myself to begin my descent. Each step on the rickety stairs gave a loud squeak that made my heart pound and skin tingle. My flashlight continued to guide me down the steps, but the further down I went, the more it seemed that the darkness was getting thicker. Was that even possible? *It's all in your head.*

By the time I reached the bottom of the steps, my nerves were rattled. Imogen had better be down here, and she better be ready to go. I was done playing these stupid games.

An awful smell rose on my left. I turned my light to it. On top of an old wooden table was an ornate black lantern. Wisps of black smoke came off it, but no light. I gave a good sniff and instantly recoiled.

Who lit this terrible thing? This was ten times worse than the stinky candles Mom lit every year. I plugged my nose and gave the contents of the lantern another glance. Inside was a grey-looking candle with weird flecks of black stuff molded inside of it. My nose crinkled. Whatever it was, I didn't care. I needed to find Immy.

I turned back around to the rest of the basement. "Immy? *Immy!*" I shouted. I thought I heard a scuffle up ahead, so I shined my light that way.

Numerous toys littered the floor and old furniture covered with large white sheets took up most of the space in the basement. Something about the odd shapes the unwanted stuff created creeped me out, but I couldn't bring myself to leave. I stood still, listening in the darkness. Was that ... breathing? It was faint, but what else did I have to go off of?

I maneuvered around a cluster of covered couches, wiping my sweaty palms on my pants as I ventured towards the back. Ahead of me were small rows of sheeted items, but one stood out to me, one particularly little-girl shaped.

I smirked. *Nice try, Immy.*

I crept up on my toes, and as soon as I was within arm's reach, I yanked the white sheet away. "Aha!" It was a rusty standing birdcage. *But I could've sworn ... Damn it!* I kicked the nearest couch and wandered aimlessly to vent off my frustration.

What could I do to draw Immy out? Talking to her wasn't working; I'd already tried that. I could try the candy route, but the bucket was all the way upstairs and she could hide again by the time I got back. I supposed I could knock stuff around until she emerged, but then I'd have to clean it all up or Mom and Dad would kill me. I walked up to an uncovered desk and wiped my finger along the top, inspecting the layer of dust on my forefinger. Maybe I could scare her out.

Suddenly, something grabbed my ankle from under the desk. I shrieked and yanked my leg back as my heart pounded. Imogen emerged from under the desk and waved at me. "Greggie, it's me."

Heat surged to my face, and I had to restrain myself from throwing the nearest thing at her. "What the heck is wrong with you? Why are you hiding down here? You know we're not allowed."

My little sister got up to her feet, then stared down at them sheepishly, but I was still pissed. This entire night was ruined because of her.

"Do you know how much trouble you've been? I can't even do what Mom and Dad told me to because you have to have your way. First you wanna play dressup," I said, mimicking her whiny voice. "Then you run around the house and I have to chase you down." I pointed to the growing bump on my forehead. "And now you want to play hide-and-seek in the basement, which you know Mom and Dad don't allow. Are you out of your freaking mind?"

Imogen looked up at me with tears in her eyes and began to sob. "I ... I'm sorry, Greggie." She hugged me then, wrapping her tiny arms around my waist and burying her face in my chest.

The angry heat drained from my face. *Crap.* Maybe I was a little too hard on her. I mean, Mom always reminded me what a nasty little crapper I'd been when I was her age. I peeled her off me, knelt down, and looked into her eyes.

"I'm sorry, Immy. You know I love you, right?"

She stopped crying and nodded her head.

"You just scared me running off like that. What if something happened to you? You're the only little sister I have."

I heard a loud knock coming from upstairs and huffed out my irritation. Screw the trick-or-treaters; this was more important.

"Listen, why don't we go back upstairs and play dressup?"

Immy's eyes lit up. "Really? Anything I want? You'll play too?"

I smiled. "Yep, whatever you want."

My little sister gave me another hug, then started skipping around me in circles . As much as I wanted to hate the idea, playing dress up was always something my little sister and me enjoyed. And anything that got me out of this dingy basement seemed like paradise at this point.

I reached my hand out to Immy and she took it, swinging it back and forth as we walked back to the stairs. As we started our ascent, I could still hear the knocks at the door upstairs. They were a lot louder now. *Christ, give it a rest. It's just candy.*

Though I was annoyed with whoever was banging at the door, in some strange way I was grateful to know that Immy and I weren't alone.

Call me a scaredy cat all you want, but there was always something about the basement that I didn't like. It always made me feel like I was being watched, like there was something in the shadows just waiting for me to make a wrong move. Even now, the frigid air crept over me, creating more goosebumps on my arms and legs. I quickened my strides up the stairs, Imogen dragging behind.

We were halfway up the stairs when the knocks stopped. For a moment, I stopped my climb. The house was eerily quiet, and for reasons I can't explain I felt a sudden urge to hurry back upstairs. I charged forward, trying to pull Immy along with me, but she resisted.

"Too fast!" she whined.

"If you hurry, we can play dress up sooner, now come on!" I yanked on Immy's arm, practically lifting her into the air. Seven steps. Just seven more steps and we could look back on this night and laugh it off. Seven, six, five. *Almost there.*

I was just three steps away from the door when I leaped for the landing. I'll never forget that jump. Time seemed to stand still, as if those cold icy fingers in the air had somehow found a way to slow time down. I remember that I had a smile on my face, a smile that disappeared when the door slammed shut in my face.

I cried out as I barrelled into the door and was flung back on the rickety steps, barely missing my little sister.

Immy hovered over me. "Greggie, you okay?"

I cursed under my breath, clutching at the bump on my head that would be doubly bruised come morning. "No, I'm not okay!" I sighed and propped myself up with a hand. "Try the door."

Imogen hopped up the last few stairs and tried the knob. It didn't budge.

"It's not mov--"

"I know," I interrupted. "Wait a sec, let me try." I groaned as I got up to my feet and walked to the door. I wrapped a hand around the knob and pushed. Nothing. I tried again, this time ramming my shoulder against the door at the same time. It didn't move at all.

But that was impossible! The door was unlocked when we came down here. No one else was in the house, so it was impossible for someone to have closed the door and locked it. What else could it be? My heart pounded at the possibilities. Ghosts. Demons. Evil creatures in the shadows. But those were just in the movies. None of it was real, right?

My little sister's eyes were big, round saucers now. "What's going on? Why can't we go upstairs?"

Crap, what was I supposed to tell her? That we were stuck in the basement? That something was down here, and it didn't want us to leave? *Grow up,* I told myself. Mom and Dad wouldn't have trusted me with this if they still thought I was scared of monsters under my bed.

I pinched the bridge of my nose with two fingers. "I don't know, Immy, but we've got to find another way. We have to go back downstairs."

I grabbed my flashlight and illuminated the way back down, grabbing Immy's hand. This time as we descended the stairs, something had changed. In addition to the hairs on my body standing up, I couldn't shake the feeling that we were being watched. The air itself seemed different, lighter, almost as if it were holding its breath, waiting for something to happen.

Imogen pulled at my hand. "I'm scared, Greggie."

I gulped. "It's gonna be okay, I promise."

As we continued down the stairs, my mind raced. There weren't any doors leading outside from down here, and even if there was a key to the upstairs, I wouldn't know where to begin searching for it. We'd have to tear the whole place apart.

We reached the basement landing, and almost immediately, my little sister started screaming.

I knelt beside her and covered her mouth, shushing her before releasing my hand. "What is it?"

She bounced up and down and squeaked as she pointed behind me.

I turned around to see what she was so scared of, and my heart nearly exploded out of my chest. On the vacant wall in front of us, an old wooden door I'd never seen before was suddenly there. The rotted vertical planks that made its rectangular shape were grey with age, almost white. Tiny plumes of a black, smoke-like substance came out from under the door.

For a moment I stood there, stunned.

"What are we gonna do?" my sister asked.

I shook my head slowly, eyes fixed on the strange door. How had it gotten here? What was behind it? Why was this even happening?

My little sister pinched me hard.

"Ow!" I yelped, coming back to my senses. "Knock it off, will ya? I'm trying to think."

I glanced around the basement for several moments when my eyes caught a slight reflection of light. Over in the far corner of the room was a window. It looked small from where I was, but at this point I'd take any escape I could get. "Immy, see that window over there? We may be able to get out that way."

Imogen shook her head and pointed. "But the door!"

I grabbed her hand and pulled it down gently. "I know, it doesn't belong here. I can't tell you how it got here or what's behind it, but I'm not gonna let anything get you, you hear me? Let's get out of here."

Imogen nodded, and I inspected the space, wondering if I could keep my promise to her. One thing was sure: we'd have to pass that strange door if we were going to get to the window. Luckily there was about ten feet between the door and the opposite wall, but it didn't leave a lot of room for mistakes. And if the door opened when we passed by ...

My eyes focused back on the strange door and the small clouds of blackness that emerged from underneath. Doors didn't just randomly appear out of thin air. There had to be a reason it had come right here, right now ...

A loud knock from upstairs interrupted my thoughts, and I blessed whoever had come by our house for bringing me back to my senses. We didn't have any time to waste; we had to get out of here before anything else happened.

I looked to my little sister. She was visibly shaking now, and I put my cold hands on the sides of her face. "Hey, we've got to keep it together, okay? I know you're scared, but we have to help each other out right now."

Imogen shot me a confusing expression that I took for bravery. *Good enough.*

"Alright, on three we're going to pass that door. We'll sidestep past it on the opposite wall. If anything happens, run towards the basement window over there and don't look back. Ready?"

"Three."

"Two."

"One!"

We crept along the opposing wall at a snail's pace, more out of fear than anything else. Imogen was in front of me. The knocking upstairs continued, but now I could hear escalating voices along with it. *Get a life,* I thought to myself. So we didn't answer the door. What were the trick-or-treaters going to do? Burn the house down?

We came upon the strange door fast, and just a few feet away from being directly across from it, my little sister stopped. She stared over at the door with an expression of such horror it made my heart ache. I reached out and touched her arm gently. She glanced over at me, her eyes so dilated they looked black.

"It's okay," I whispered. "Keep going." I motioned in the direction we were headed with my flashlight.

Imogen inched along as I watched with bated breath. But nothing happened, and once she was clear of the door she scampered away as fast as she could. I breathed a sigh of relief and readied myself. It was my turn.

I followed Imogen's lead across the wall in slow, steady footsteps, but when I was directly across from the door, the knocking upstairs suddenly stopped. All was quiet in the house again, and my hairs stood on end so much I was surprised they didn't shoot off into the air of their own accord. I forced myself to continue onward, but an abrupt groan from the door made me freeze. I shined my light on it from the bottom up.

Smoke continued to billow from the base of the door, but now small holes in the rotted wooden planks began to emit the strange substance too. As my light reached eye level, I saw two yellow points of light appear behind cracks in the wood. It was almost like they were watching me. The door groaned again, this time shocking me into action. I broke off in a sprint, running as fast as I could to the far corner of the basement.

The second time the door moaned I'd seen the yellow lights move. Whatever was there, it was alive, and I wasn't about to look back and check it out again. We had to get out. *Now*.

I ran to the furthest edge of the basement, my light bobbing up and down as I went. Imogen was jumping up and down trying to reach the latch on the window, but it was just out of reach for her.

"Here, let me," I huffed, out of breath. I handed her my flashlight. "Shine it on the window so I can get a better look."

Imogen flashed the light on the window's bottom edge. Orange-red-brown rust covered the latch and outer edges, and it seemed like no one had ever used this window before, maybe even since the house had first been built. I tried the latch. It wouldn't budge.

"Damn it!" I cursed.

"What's wrong?" Imogen asked.

"There's rust all over this stupid thing. I'm gonna have to

find something to break the latch, either that or bust the window open."

I took the flashlight and dared a glance at her, but was really checking on the damned door behind her. It was still closed, but the smoke coming from it was now flowing out in thick streams. *Shit.*

"I've got to find something to bust that latch open with. While I'm doing that, will you keep an eye on that door? I know it's scary, but I need to know if it opens, even the slightest bit."

Imogen frowned. "O-okay," she mumbled.

I placed a hand on her shoulder gently. "I'm not going to let anything happen to you, Immy. Just shout if something happens and I'll come running." I shoved the flashlight back into her hands and stalked off, cursing my rotten luck.

I shuffled blindly betweens columns of furniture and old boxes, groping along the items to steady myself. *Come on, come on. Think! Where is something I can use?*

The only things Mom ever put down here was old clothes and jewelry that wasn't 'in season' anymore. I rustled through the first few boxes around me, finding odd knick knacks, summer clothes, and some old VHS tapes. *Damn it!*

I breathed hard. What about Dad? When was the last time I had been down here with him? There had to be something ... *Wait, that's it!* Dad quit playing golf at the beginning of the year. I had helped him tow his duffel bag of golf clubs down here. But where?

I tried to relive my memory. Dad had talked about how one day I could try golfing out myself as we walked down the basement stairs. We went right; I remember how brightly the sun shone through the small basement window. I actually had to shield my face for a moment. We made our way around the back side of the wall and I made fun of an old sofa that looked like it was made for grannies. Dad said it belonged to his mom and got this funny look on his face, then he took the duffel bag, shoved it under the couch, and we went back upstairs.

The couch couldn't be far from here, but now everything was covered in those stupid white sheets. I yanked up the nearest sheet-covered furniture, inspecting it.

"Greggie!" Immy screamed.

"Hold on, I think I may have something!"

I doubled my pace, nearly tripping over myself as my heart thundered in my ears. *Oh god, oh god, oh god.* If I didn't hurry, something might happen to Imogen. Damn it, why didn't I bring her with me?

After what felt like an eternity, I found the couch. I fell to the floor and pulled out the duffel bag from under the sofa with a grunt. It was a lot heavier than I remembered. I wouldn't be able to take the whole thing with me.

"The door's opening!" my little sister wailed.

"Coming!" I unzipped the duffel bag and took the first golf club I could get my hands on. Luckily, it had a big head, good for beating that latch or clobbering whatever was behind the door into submission.

I sprinted down the columns of towering boxes and unwanted items, praying that I would get back to my little sister in time. When I turned the last corner I froze completely.

A few feet away from Imogen was a tall, towering figure.

It was clad in black, tattered robes and a long hood masked its face. It was bent over, staring into her eyes and pointing extremely long, spindly fingers at her face.

I gawked at the otherworldly figure in front of me. *What the hell is that?* It had to be at least eight feet tall at standing height. And why wasn't Imogen running? She looked ... angry.

"No!" Imogen cried, stomping her foot with her eyebrows furrowed.

The monster tilted its hooded head for a moment, then an inhumanly high-pitched screech erupted from it. The walls themselves seemed to vibrate from the force of it. The ghastly sound boomed through me, and I nearly dropped my golf club. That thing ... it wasn't human. God, how were we going to get out of here alive?

Without warning, the monster snatched my little sister up with its large skeletal fingers. Imogen screeched. She twisted and turned violently before we locked eyes.

"Greggie, help!"

The monster began carrying Imogen away.

My blood went cold. How was I supposed to help my sister? How could I hurt this, this *thing*? Would it kill me? A little pee trickled down my pants.

"Greggie!"

Hearing the fear in my sister's voice again snapped me out of my paralysis. It didn't matter what happened to me. Immy was in trouble, and I had to save her, even from this mammoth of a beast.

I scrambled after them. They were about halfway to the door by the time I caught up to them.

"Hey, asshole!" I shouted. The tall monster turned around, its yellow eyes ogling me. "Let my sister go right now!"

The monster stared at me for a moment, then it was right in my face. The odor coming from it was so awful my eyes started tearing up. It was like burnt rotten food thrown in a dirty diaper.

The same inhuman wail came from under its hood, only up this close I felt my entire body quake from the force. I closed my eyes out of fear, but when I opened them the monster was continuing its journey back to the strange door, Imogen trapped in one of its large bony hands.

I clenched my jaw. That bastard wanted to take my sister away from me, to do God knew what to her. I wasn't going to let that happen without a fight. I charged at the monster full speed. "Give. Her. Back!"

I lifted the golf club above my head and smashed it on the beast's back. It gave a horrible shriek of pain, then spun around faster than I could react. The next thing I knew, I was flying in the air until my body smacked against the concrete wall of the basement.

Numb with pain, I groped around my head blindly. It was wet from where it had hit the wall. I tried to think, but my head pounded in dull throbs.

Imogen!

I glanced around as best I could. The monster was opening the strange door, Imogen still in its grasp.

"Greggie, help!" Imogen begged. "Please don't let him take me away!"

"Immy!" I shouted.

I tried to get up, but my body wouldn't budge. I was too beaten and sore. I struck my legs with my fists, but it was no use. So I did the only thing I could think of in that state. I cried like a baby as my sister and the monster disappeared behind the strange door.

CHAPTER 3

I walked through the field I always took home from school, still in shock as I reread the letter the principal demanded I take home to my parents. Suspended? *Suspended?* The fight wasn't even my fault! I threw down my arms and winced at the pain that echoed through my body. I wanted to scream at the top of my lungs, to break or hurt something. Wasn't it bad enough that my sister was taken from me? Now I'd have to explain my black eye and bruises to Mom and Dad.

I scoffed to myself. *Like they'd believe that either.*

It had only been several weeks since Immy disappeared, and already my life was turning to shit.

By the time my parents got home on Halloween night, I was sitting on the porch out of my mind. I'd passed out in the basement and woke up to find the strange door still there with no sign of the monster or Immy. I was so terrified that I burst through the window and pulled myself out of there.

When they asked me what happened I tried telling them the truth, but of course they didn't buy my crazy story. Mom and Dad stormed through the house, searching every nook and cranny for Immy, but she wasn't anywhere. I told them to look in the basement; though the strange door was gone, they observed the unlocked basement door and broken glass by the window with an excuse for everything.

If I didn't find the key to the basement door, then Immy did, and I was a neglectful brother. The broken glass was obviously due to an intruder breaking in. And my injuries, well, sure I could've tried to fight off the kidnapper, but they didn't really care at that point.

Mom went into hysterics, yelling at me for being so careless, so stupid and inattentive. Dad simply went mute, like he'd never spoken a word in his life. My parents called the police, but I already knew how that would go.

The police and search parties couldn't find Immy. Shortly after that, the whole town was in an uproar when the FBI rolled in. They said something about recurring child disappearances over the past few decades. I was shocked and hopeful when they arrived, but even they came up short.

My sister's disappearance made the local news. The nearby TV Station even had an interview with Dad; Mom couldn't talk about Immy for more than a few seconds without getting emotional. I tried telling the reporter the truth, but the second I mentioned a monster he laughed and Dad apologized for having a kid with such an 'overactive imagination.' Instead, I was typecast as a careless big brother who didn't give two craps about his family. You can imagine how a small town like mine ate that up.

School got worse every day. The other kids gave me dirty looks, elbowed me in the halls, or pushed me into lockers. I tried to maintain my innocence, but things just kept getting worse. Today I finally snapped and punched one of my tormentors in the face. I just couldn't take it anymore. And now here I was, walking home in shame.

The end of the field was just ahead. I readied myself to cross the road to my street, and a car approached. As it neared, the backseat windows rolled down. I recognized the ugly faces of two of the bullies at school that had been giving me all kinds of hell.

"Sister killer, sister killer!" they screamed.

One of them hurled something at me before they sped by. I couldn't tell what it was until the Big Gulp exploded all over me, drenching me from head to toe.

I fell to the ground with a thud, tears already in my eyes. I screamed at myself and slapped my face. Why was I such a damn baby? I was weak. Nobody cared what had happened. No one thought about my sister. I was all alone.

I sat up and wrapped my arms around my knees, burying my face in them as I sobbed. What was I supposed to do? I couldn't move on without Immy. She was my baby sister. I was supposed to protect her, and I'd failed. An image of my little sister defying the monster flashed in my mind.

My tears stopped. I had to be strong like Immy. I couldn't keep feeling sorry for myself. I had two options now. I could either let what that monster did go or I could stand up and figure it out for myself. I wiped at my eyes, stood up, and grabbed my backpack. I would find my sister and bring her back. There had to be a way.

I stood at the edge of the field for a moment, thinking on what to do. Immy had gone missing. Should I tell the FBI my story? I shook my head. I doubt they'd listen to my crazy story about a monster in the basement and take me seriously. The reporter hadn't.

No, there had to be something else. Wait, they ran reports on kids that went missing, didn't they? Maybe there was information I hadn't seen, something that could lead me back to her. Whatever the case, the library was a good starting place. Still, I hesitated. The library was a few miles from here. Too long to walk there and back. I'd have to stop home and grab my bike.

I crossed the street and walked up my driveway. For some odd reason, my parents were already home. Curious, I was just about to walk in when the weight of the now-soggy letter from the principal in my hand drew my attention.

If I went inside, I'd have to explain what happened. Would they really let me go to the library right after getting suspended from school? I backed away from the front door and peeked inside one of the windows looking into the dining room.

Mom was sitting at the table with Dad. She was laughing about something and seemed totally fine. Dad looked like his former self, cheerful even. They leaned across the table for a kiss, and I left the window with a bitter taste in my mouth.

What was wrong with my parents? Immy had only been gone a few weeks, and they were moving on like nothing happened. How could they sit around gabbing when she might still be alive?

I snuck around to the backyard and sped over to the library on my bike. When I walked in, old Mrs. Greeley the librarian greeted me. She was a walking cliche, from her horn-rimmed glasses and tight bun all the way to her shoulder-padded jacket and knee-length skirt.

She was a lot older than most of these books, but was always nice to me. She helped show me where to find recent newspaper copies that may have further updates on Immy's search as well as the catalog of missing children's reports.

I started researching the newspapers and the most recent report that included Immy, but my heart sunk when I didn't find anything helpful. I wanted to stop right there, but something told me to keep going.

I continued reading over other missing children's reports from the past few years, and that's when I began to see similarities between Immy's disappearance and theirs.

Almost every year around fall time, a couple of kids went missing in town. Most of them had been around my age, but in some cases a younger kid vanished. In all of the missing children reports, each kid disappeared when they were left home alone or with a sibling. It didn't make any sense. Why were kids going missing every year? Obviously whatever this monster was, it preyed around this time of year. But that didn't explain how this was happening in the first place or why the FBI hadn't figured it out by now.

I tried to look further into the articles I'd read, but

none of the parents or surviving children had said anything more than that their kid or sibling was gone. There were follow-up articles on the search party efforts and FBI involvement, but in time each case was called off with no results. It was bizarre. What was really going on here?

I was nearly going crossed-eyed poring over more articles and reports when I flipped over an especially dull page. A small newspaper cutout flew out onto the floor, and I bent over to pick it up.

According to the brief article, a little kid named Danny went missing four years ago. Unlike the other reports I'd read, this one said that his big brother Trent kept insisting that a beast had taken his brother from their basement.

My heart pounded in my chest. This Trent kid may have seen what I'd seen before Immy was taken away. Could he know something more than I did? Would he be willing to tell me what happened? I read over the article three more times, jotting down the most important details. Luckily the story gave his last name, which was an odd one at that: Duffie.

There were only two Duffies in the library's phone book. The first number didn't answer, but when the second one picked up, I was overjoyed.

"Duffie residence," a slightly older woman's voice said impatiently.

"Um, hi. I'm looking for Trent Duffie."

I could hear the woman breathing on the line, but she didn't respond, so I pulled for the best lie I could think of.

"Sorry, my name's Michael. I'm a former classmate of his

and he told me if I ever needed notes on geometry class to give him a call."

"Trent doesn't live here anymore," the woman snapped.

Puzzled, I couldn't think of anything to say.

"He emancipated himself two years ago. Surely if you were a good friend of his, you would know that."

Emancipated? What did that even mean? "I, I-I'm sorry, I'm just trying to get this project done by tomorrow. It's really important."

"Don't call here again." The line went dead.

My stomach dropped. There went my lead. How the heck was I supposed to find Trent now? My town wasn't that big, but I was just one person. Finding him would be impossible on my own. Defeated, I grabbed my backpack and sulked towards the entrance.

"Gregory," a familiar voice called.

I spun around. It was old Mrs. Greeley again. "Yes, Mrs. Greeley?" I asked politely.

"I couldn't help but hear your conversation."

"Oh," I muttered. "I know I'm not supposed to use the phone without asking, but I--"

Mrs. Greeley put up a hand, silencing me. "Nothing is more important than your education, young man. The lengths you went to in an attempt to learn are admirable." She smiled toothily and handed me a small folded piece of paper. "Trent Duffie works at Steve's Autobody. You'll find directions on that sheet of paper."

I could've kissed her I was so happy. "Wow, thank you so much!"

"Think nothing of it. Now go and learn."

"Will do." I started walking away when something ran through my mind. I turned around. "Mrs. Greeley?"

"Yes, Gregory?"

"What's it mean to emancipate yourself?"

Mrs. Greeley made an awkward face, then trudged off as fast as she could.

CHAPTER 4

Twenty minutes later, I arrived at the autobody shop. Mrs. Greeley's directions took me to the other side of town a few miles away. Well-kept suburban homes had given way to run-down apartment buildings and houses that were little more than shacks. Trash littered the potholed streets, and I had to steer wildly to avoid both as I approached on my bike.

When I got to the front side of the building, Steve's Autobody was spelled out in faded red and white letters. The walls had a thick layer of grime that hadn't been attended to in years. *Charming.*

I parked my bike on the building's side facing away from the street to avoid unnecessary attention. At first I considered going through the front door, but decided against it. If anyone asked why I was there, they probably wouldn't buy whatever excuse I'd come up with to see Trent. Lying obviously wasn't my strong suit based on my phone call with Mrs. Duffie.

Instead, I walked around back to where the work was being done, following the echoed clangs, buzzes, and ratcheting sounds. Three vehicles were currently being worked on in little divided areas. To the far right, a stocky middle-aged man with very little hair on his head was kneeling on the driver's side of a beat up jeep. In the middle slot, a younger guy with a lankier build was wiping his sweaty forehead with a filthy rag. I couldn't be sure, but something told me he was a little too old to be Trent. I glanced over the spot closest to me.

Poking out from under a rusty station wagon were a pair of legs. The shoes were beat up, but definitely something someone younger would wear. I tried to get a glimpse of the guy underneath, but if I leaned forward any more I would risk exposing my presence to the other employees. I darted over to the station wagon as quietly as I could and tapped the guy's legs.

"Hey!" I heard the guy shout from underneath.

The man slid out from under the car and glared up at me. His rusty brown hair shot out in every direction, and he had grease stains all over his face. "What do you want kid? Lose your parents?"

"No, I was looking for you. You're Trent Duffie, right?"

"Yeah, what's it to you?"

"I wanted to talk to you about your brother Danny."

Trent grimaced and got to his feet, cleaning off his oily hands with a rag.

The silence was deafening, and I was beginning to get really nervous. Had I approached this all wrong? Would he even tell me anything? This was my one chance. Damn it, I should've thought this through more.

The middle-aged guy from two slots down noticed me and approached fast. He didn't look happy. "Beat it kid, we've got work to do."

Trent put up a hand. "It's okay, Mel. I'm due for a break anyway."

Mel frowned. "Five minutes."

Trent led the way back where I'd parked my bike, but as soon as we turned the corner, he pinned me against the brick wall, the hard edges biting into my back. "Who sent you?" he asked, his face contorted in a snarl.

"W-what are you talking about?"

He pressed his forearm against my neck; it was getting hard to breathe. "I said who!" he hissed.

"Nobody sent me, I swear!" I croaked. "My s-sister went missing a month back, just like your ... ungh, little brother four years ago. I thought you could help."

Trent eased off me a little, and I took in a deep breath of air. "How the hell did you find me?" he asked.

"I found an old newspaper article at the library. Please, you've got to help me. I have to find my sister before it's too late."

Trent scoffed and let me go. He pulled out a pack of cigarettes and lit one up, blowing a cloud of smoke in my face. I coughed a little bit.

"I can't help you," he said. "And even if I could, it's too late for your sister."

"Why can't you? And what do you mean it's too late?

Trent flicked his cigarette. Several small embers dropped

to the ground before they fizzled out. "Listen kid, why don't you just move on with your life? Save us both some trouble."

I clenched my fists. "No, I can't let this go. I think ... no, I know something's going on around here."

Trent took another drag of his cigarette. "Oh yeah? And what's that?"

I stared at the ground, trying to assemble whatever theories I'd formed from the past couple weeks. "I don't know, it almost seems like ... look, I just know there's something happening behind all this. I can't explain it."

Trent's expression went serious as he took another drag. "Sorry kid, I'm busy here."

Mel came around the corner, glancing at both of us suspiciously. "Say goodbye to your little friend here, time to get back to work."

Trent stomped out his cigarette and started to follow after Mel without saying anything, but I lunged forward and grabbed the back of his shirt.

"Hey, don't just walk away! You've got to help me."

Trent snatched back his shirt and eyed me with disgust. "Listen, you little brat. I don't have to do anything. I'm an adult. I have responsibilities. I don't have time to talk to you all day about this crap. If you really care about your sister, why don't you prove it and stop wasting my time?"

Trent pulled a torn piece of paper out of his pocket, scribbled something on it, and thrust it at me before leaving. I scrambled after it just before it fell into a nearby puddle. It was a phone number with his name written underneath. After a quick glance in Trent's direction, I went back to my bike and headed home.

How was I supposed to figure this out on my own? Trent hadn't given me any information except that it was too late for Immy. My vision blurred with tears at the thought. Could it really be true? Was she gone forever?

I shook my head and wiped at my eyes. *Don't get emotional.*

I focused on my conversation with Trent. He knew more than he was letting on. He didn't completely reject the crazy story I told him like everyone else had, but he was also hesitant to say anything, almost like he was holding back. Why?

I remembered what he'd first said to me. He was worried that someone had sent me to find him. But why would he worry about that? The monster or monsters that took our siblings weren't capable of that, were they? An otherworldly shriek echoed in my head and I cringed.

So then who was Trent afraid of? Someone else had to know something, but as hard as I tried, I couldn't think of anyone. Still, one thing was certain. Trent gave me his number for a reason. He wouldn't give me the information I wanted free and clear, but based on his last words to me, if I could get some information myself he might be willing to talk, maybe explain why no one was able to locate all these missing kids.

As I rolled into my driveway, I decided to continue monitoring my parents. Their quick recovery from Immy's disappearance was the only thing so far that stuck out to me as truly odd, and if they were involved somehow I would know in time. I just hoped that it would be soon enough, for Immy's sake.

CHAPTER 5

couple of days went by, and I continued watching my parents. My suspension was over, but I got home from school before them so I wouldn't miss a thing. At first everything seemed normal, better even. Mom and Dad got home. They made dinner and included me in their conversations. I even suffered their awful new routine of daily family game nights.

But there was something different in their expressions when they looked at me. Their eyes seemed more cold and calculating, like they were analyzing me. Sure, they still smiled, but it never reached their eyes like it used to. They'd never looked at me this way before, and it freaked me out. What was the cause of this sudden change? Were they upset with me? Did they suspect I was monitoring them?

Regardless of my conflicting thoughts and emotions, I went along with my plan and played the part of a 'good son.' If I wanted to discover the source of my parents' oddness, I'd have to play it safe. Besides, it was pretty easy to fake it given the glaring example right in front of me.

On the third night of observing my parents, I finally made a break. I'd gone to the laundry room to look around when my heart stopped. On top of the dryer in a laundry basket was my little sister's favorite outfit folded neatly. I grabbed the smiley face shirt softly and pressed it to my chest. *Immy.*

Overcome with emotion, I ran upstairs, closed my bedroom door, and turned off the light. I closed my eyes hoping for sleep, but my mind was racing. I hadn't seen anything of Imogen's since she disappeared. What were Mom and Dad doing with her stuff? Would they give it away? She hadn't even been gone for more than a month!

Calm down, I told myself. I didn't know anything just yet. I'd just have to wait and see.

Over the next few days, my suspicions were confirmed. Not only were more of Immy's clothes being folded into neat piles, but her personal items were being gathered up in little plastic bags. I couldn't believe it.

This was really happening. My parents were erasing every trace of my little sister. But why? They didn't know what had happened. Unless ... could they possibly know about the monster that came for us on Halloween night? Even if they did, their reaction didn't make any sense. They'd ignored what I told them the night it happened. They didn't alert the town of the monster's presence. No, they'd made me look like an idiot instead.

A clatter downstairs interrupted my thoughts. I snuck from my sunlit room to the edge of the upper landing. I couldn't see my dad, but Mom was standing in front of the basement entry with the door open.

"I put it in the box labelled 'Photo Albums'," she whispered loudly to my dad, annoyance in her voice.

What were they talking about? They hardly ever went into the basement, and I doubted anything of Immy's was down there.

"I can't find it!" Dad called up to her.

"*Christ*," Mom growled to herself, swiping a wavy strand of brown hair behind her ear. "I'm coming down."

Seeing an opportunity, I crept down the stairs as quietly as possible. I had to know what they were looking for, especially if it led me to Immy. A brief moment later, my parents' footsteps echoed loudly on the rickety steps as they came back up, and I darted into the kitchen out of sight.

"I don't know how you couldn't find it, I told you where it was," Mom said. "God, this thing reeks."

I dared a glance around the corner. Mom was holding the grey, smelly candle in the lantern that I'd found the night my little sister was taken. What was she doing with it?

"Yes, but it did the job, didn't it?" Dad said. "At least when we give it back to the priest we won't have to deal with this again."

I gawked at my parents. What in the world was going on here? 'Did the job.' What did that mean? And since when did they talk to a priest? We'd never been a church family. I tried to find some strange reason that a priest would give them the odd, stinky candle but I couldn't. Somehow this had to do with Immy, I just knew it.

"I'll go check on Gregory, you gather Imogen's stuff,"

Dad said. He moved towards the landing, but Mom barred his way with her free arm.

"Wait, I think he fell asleep in his room. Why bother him? Get her things from the laundry room, I'll call for him and make sure he's asleep."

Dad walked over to the laundry room, and Mom peered up the landing in my room's direction, going up a step. "Gregory, we're going grocery shopping," she called softly. "Do you want anything? Pizza rolls?"

I flattened myself against the kitchen wall, holding my breath.

"Hmm, guess not."

I heard a shuffle and risked a glance around the corner again. Dad had a large bundle of Immy's clothes under one arm and several plastic bags in his other hand. "Well?"

"He's asleep, just like I thought. Come on, let's go."

As soon as I heard the front door shut, I bolted for the back door. Mom and Dad were up to something, and I'd be damned if they were going to just drop off Immy's stuff and wipe their hands clean of her. I had to find out who this priest was and what was so important about that strange candle. I ran outside and grabbed my bike, then edged up the side of my house cautiously.

My parents' car revved to life and drove off, and I waited a couple seconds before mounting my bike and following them. I stayed under tree cover and out of their rear view range as much as possible, but keeping up with them on top of that was nearly impossible. At first my parents headed in the direction of the local Goodwill, but a mile later we passed it without stopping.

After nearly losing my parents several times through sudden twists and turns, I followed them into an area of town that resembled the neighborhood where Trent worked – abandoned houses, forgotten business buildings, trash-littered streets. Finally, my parents parked in a potholed lot next to a plain-looking two-story building.

I stashed my bike behind some overgrown bushes and watched them exit the car and go inside. I had to follow them, but I hesitated. Was I really about to do this? What if they caught me? There'd be no turning back from this.

Trent's words echoed inside my head. *If you really care about your sister, why don't you prove it?* I clenched my fists. He was right. I could either let my parents bury my sister and forget her, or I could man up and find out the truth. Immy deserved that.

I ran across the small parking lot and opened the door, closing it softly behind me. Inside, the building was eerily quiet. Luckily, no one was in the bare hallway that stretched in two directions. In front of me, the hallway rounded and ended at a set of double doors, not unlike those a typical church would have. To my left, a number of small rooms dotted the hall. Under one of the doors fluorescent light was visible, so I edged closer, hoping that no one would come charging down the hall and see me.

As I neared the door, I recognized the voices from within: my parents. I leaned as close to the door as I dared.

"Thank you for seeing us on such short notice," my dad said.

"Think nothing of it," an elderly voice said, the priest I assumed. "How have you been coping with your loss?"

"I ... we..." A strange cry erupted from my mom. "It's still really hard for me. Some days all I can think of is Imogen, how she was. How she was so full of life."

"Oh, honey," Dad said in an empathetic tone.

"May I be frank?" the priest said. "What you are experiencing is completely normal after a loss like this. It's only natural for families in your situation to miss the deceased, wish they were still here with us. But with our Order comes great responsibility, and even greater reward. Your sacrifice does not go unnoticed. Have you brought the lantern?"

Deceased? Sacrifice? What was this geezer talking about, and what did it have to do with that stupid lantern? I leaned closer.

"Y-yes," Mom stuttered, followed by a brief clang.

"Um, what about the other terms of our deal?" Dad said.

"Ah, yes. You will be granted immunity for the next ten years. And as severance goes, please accept this check on our behalf. I think you will find it fitting."

"This is ... honey, look!" Dad said, shock and awe in his voice.

"Oh my goodness. I can't believe it! With this we--"

"Should be able to live comfortably," the priest completed my Mom's sentence.

A loud squeal of excitement came from my parents, and I backed away from the door with a sour taste in my mouth. I couldn't believe what I was hearing. My parents had been working with the priest and this 'Order' to get rid of my sister. And when they succeeded they were being *rewarded* for it? My vision blurred as I teared up. My parents were the real monsters.

I bolted outside and mounted my bike, but stopped myself. What was I supposed to do? My parents had caused Immy's disappearance. I couldn't go home, but where else could I go? Who could I even trust anymore? I clutched my head with my fists. God, why was this happening to me?

An image of Trent throwing a torn slip of paper at me flashed through my mind. *That's right, he gave me his number.* But could I really rely on him? The more I went about searching for answers, the more it seemed that I was on my own. Still, Trent hadn't given me any true reason to doubt him. He didn't not believe my story, and he hadn't spilled the beans to anyone else. As much as I hated to admit it, he was my best hope.

I sighed and pedaled to the nearest pay phone.

———

MY PULSE THUNDERED in my ears as the ringback tone rang once, twice, three times. Finally, Trent answered.

"Yeah, what is it?" he asked.

I froze. *Oh god, what should I say?* That my parents were responsible for my sister's disappearance and I needed help? That they were the real monsters? That I had nowhere to go? I tried to form words, but instead an odd squeak came out from the back of my throat.

"I, I-I ... My p-parents," I managed to croak.

"Are you the kid who came by my work last week?"

"Y-yes!" I stammered. "Please help me! My parents, they ... they lied to me. My s-sister, she's gone because of them."

Fresh tears ran down my cheek, and I started to wheeze. "They did this."

He cursed. "Meet me at the autobody shop in ten minutes. Don't stop by your house, just come straight here."

"Okay," I whimpered. The line went dead, and I hung up the receiver. I took in a deep breath and wiped at my eyes trying to calm myself, but I was frantic.

All this time, my parents had planned this. How long had they been preparing? How was it even possible to summon a monster? It could've taken me or Immy. Did they even care which one of us it took? How was Trent even going to protect me from them? They were still my parents, weren't they?

Stop it, I told myself. Freaking out wouldn't solve anything. I needed to head over to the autobody shop and figure this out before my parents got home. I forced myself back on my bike and pedaled as fast as I could.

By the time I reached Steve's Autobody, Trent was standing in the parking lot next to an old red pickup truck. He waved at me and I stopped my bike behind the truck. This close, his concern was evident in his crinkled forehead and raised eyebrows.

"Are you okay?"

I shook my head. The last thing I wanted was to have a mental breakdown in public, and talking about everything now would most likely put me in a frenzy again.

Trent gestured to my bike and I nodded, wheeling it to him. He raised it up into the bed of his truck.

"Where are we going?" I asked.

"We shouldn't talk about anything unless we know we're

safe and won't be heard." He walked over to the passenger side and opened the door, signaling me to get in. "I'll take you back to my place."

I stood there, unsure of myself. If I went with him, there'd be no turning back from whatever information he shared. Did I really want to know what was going on around me? Could the situation get any worse than it already was?

Trent frowned. "I'm not a perv, kid. Do you want answers or not?"

Unable to protest, I got in the car.

The drive to Trent's place wasn't far, just a couple miles west, he told me. Still, the trip there was awkward. Country music played in the background, and he kept trying to make small talk, but I didn't really know what to say.

Here I was, in some stranger's truck, who also claimed that a monster took his sibling on Halloween. Yeah, nothing weird about that at all. I did finally manage to give him my name, and soon after that we rolled up to a tiny, beaten-up house with an overgrown yard and outer siding that was falling apart.

Trent laughed when he saw the look on my face. "I know it's not much to look at, but it's home. Come on, lets go inside."

We entered the house and Trent told me to make myself comfortable as he freshened up. Old floorboards creaked under my feet as I observed his mismatched furniture and lack of decor on the walls. The kitchen was tiny, and his bedroom didn't seem much bigger than that. Still, I was pretty impressed. Trent was on his own at 18. It had to be tough living by himself.

Trent came out into the living room and sat down on a battered old couch. I followed his lead, then stared down at my feet.

"Hey, it's gonna be okay," he said.

I scoffed. "How? Everything is falling apart all around me. It's not like you can promise that anyways."

Trent frowned. "Let's not start things this way. Why don't you tell me what happened from the beginning?"

I glanced over at him. "Are you sure about this?"

"Of course. I need to know what you know. Take your time, and don't leave anything out."

"Alright." I sighed as I prepared to relive the nightmare of the past month, hoping that just maybe we could figure this whole thing out together.

CHAPTER 6

"And that's when I called you from the pay phone." I looked over at Trent, searching for any sign that he thought I was crazy. He seemed to be in some kind of trance, and his eyes were watery.

I'd spent the past thirty minutes or so telling my story, from the night of Immy's disappearance and the trouble I'd had at school afterwards to my suspicions about my parents and how they were confirmed. It felt good to finally tell someone everything, but now I was anxious.

"You think I'm insane, right?"

A strange, sad yelp came from Trent as he wiped a fresh tear from his eye. "I lost Danny the same way you lost Imogen. If you're crazy, then so am I."

I stared at him, shocked at how similar our nightmarish realities had been.

"I wasn't okay for a long time. I didn't have anyone to turn to, and my parents thought I'd lost it. All I could do was try to get away. That's why I emancipated myself when I was 16."

I gawked at him, puzzled.

"It's when you separate from your parents before you're eighteen for irreconcilable differences."

"Irreconcilable?"

Trent sighed and put a hand to his forehead. "There's so much you don't understand. You've seen some of it, but you've only scratched the surface. If you're absolutely sure, I'll tell you everything I know, but I understand if you want to bury all of this and just move on."

I thought it over for a moment. He was right. I could move on with my life. Graduate from high school, get a job, go to college, live a happy life. But all of that was without Immy. She was innocent in all of this. How many other innocent lives had been destroyed? I'd counted at least ten in my research, but there had to be more than that, much more. How could I forget her, forget the betrayal of my parents, the darkness that hovered over my town?

"Tell me everything."

Trent cleared his throat and lit up a cigarette, pulling the ashtray on the table closer to him . "After Danny was taken away from me everything fell apart, just like it did for you. I tried to tell the truth, but no one would listen to me. I started skipping school, having sex, and smoking, and my parents threatened to ship me off to military school if I didn't shape up. So I faked it, just like you did."

He took a long drag of his cigarette and blew out a cloud of smoke. "Two years went by, two long, agonizing years of hiding what I was really feeling. A growing part of me resented my parents for moving on without Danny. After a while, I started having dreams of him. He and my parents would float away from me, leading me to that damn door in the basement every time."

"At that point, I hadn't talked to my parents in six months, so I filed for emancipation. Once I was on my own, I quit school and started working at Steve's. I wanted to move on, but it wasn't enough. I kept seeing Danny and my shit parents. When I couldn't take the anger anymore, I started following my folks."

"What did you find?" I asked.

"At first, nothing. But a few weeks before Halloween, following them led me to an abandoned warehouse just outside of town. At first I thought maybe they were lost, but they seemed to know where they were going. When we got there, there were dozens of cars parked around the building. I recognized some of the cars parked, as well as some of the people getting out of their cars and going in. They were parents, Greg. I knew them from my time at the auto shop."

Questions raged inside my head, flowing out of my lips. "But what were they doing there? What do they have to do with the monsters?"

Trent took one last drag of his cigarette and snuffed it out in his ashtray. "They call it a Reaping. Every year the parents go to an undisclosed location and have a drawing. The winning family ... they have to sacrifice one of their children to the monsters we saw."

Trent eyed me intently.

What was he saying? That his family and mine were the unlucky winners of some demented lottery? No, it couldn't be. I shot up, unable to contain my emotions. "That's impossible! Why would all the parents agree to do something like that? My parents love me!"

Trent held up his hands. "Wait, I'm not saying they don't. There's more at play here than you understand. Please, sit down."

Hesitantly, I sat down, crossing my arms.

"When I eavesdropped on the meeting, they explained the situation for the new parents in attendance. According to them, since the founding of our town, there has always been a large number of disappearances. At first they thought this land was cursed, but when they found out that these monsters were lurking around, they had to find a way to stop it from happening, or at least minimize the problem."

Trent pulled out a manilla folder and handed it to me. Inside were several crumbly, decades-old newspaper clippings. I glanced them over as he continued.

"These articles are the only suggestion of the monsters I could find. I call them Reapers. Our local newspaper published the story, but as you can see, the next day they recanted, calling it a hoax. But it wasn't. People were really disappearing. So once our town was able to lower the numbers of missing persons--"

"They could justify their actions," I said, anger flowing through my veins. "But how did they control the number of disappearances?"

Trent clasped his hands together and bowed his head against them. "Have you ever noticed the number of candles being burnt around here?"

The image of my mother lighting candles at Halloween every year flashed in my mind. I slowly nodded.

"The parents use special herbs built into their candles to repel the monsters."

"Then why don't they just keep lighting the candles? Why even have a Reaping?"

"I don't know. My guess is that the herbs only work so well, otherwise there wouldn't be any more disappearances. That's why they still have the lottery, why they use the other candles."

Shock shot down my spine in cold tingles as I remembered the strange lantern creating the awful smell in the basement. If the candles my mom normally used repelled the monsters, then the other one ... "The other candle attracts them."

Trent frowned. "Yes. They must've found another set of herbs that attracted the monsters. That's what they use in the houses for those chosen for the reaping."

I nodded blankly, putting all of the details together in my head. The parents, the candles, the disappearances, it all made sense now. They used the candles to repel and attract the Reapers to prevent them from coming out whenever they wanted. Still, knowing this didn't make anything better. From my research in the library, none of the missing children had ever been found, and if the past was any proof then that meant ... I put my face in my hands, tears streaming through my fingers. "Immy's really gone, isn't she?"

I felt Trent's hand on my shoulder. "I'm so sorry, Greg."

I jolted back up, glaring at him through my blurry

vision. "Then what good is any of this? There's no way to bring Danny and Imogen back."

"We may not be able to bring them back, but there's one way to avenge Danny and Imogen, to avenge all of them."

"What?" I sniffled.

"We expose the whole damned thing."

———

I MADE my way to the front driveway from Trent's back shed, groaning as the mass of bear traps, metal chains, and a bunch of other hunting tools weighed down on me.

I hadn't needed much convincing from Trent to help him expose the truth of this town. Though I was still reeling from my loss, I wasn't going to let my sister's death be in vain. On top of that, maybe even more so, I was furious. The parents of this town and the Order commanding them had to answer for what they were doing. Regardless of how they saw things, people were still being taken, people that deserved full and happy lives. No one else would die if Trent and I could get the evidence we needed to the FBI. If anyone could stop the Reapers, it was them.

I set the traps down in the bed of the truck with a sigh and looked to Trent, who was shuffling through the contents. "So how is this going to work again?"

"For starters, we'll need one of those candles they use to attract the Reapers. Do you remember where the abandoned building your parents went is?"

I thought about it, then shook my head. "Not exactly, but I do know the general area it's in. From there we can narrow it down. But how are we going to get to that candle? What if the doors are locked?"

Trent grimaced. "You let me worry about that. Once we're inside, I'll need you to lead me to where they left it, and after that we can head to your place. Did you confirm with your parents?"

"Yeah, they said they had plans in town tonight, and I told them I was staying with a friend for the night. The house should be empty, so we can use the basement to draw out the monster." I stared down at my feet. I didn't want to give wind to my worries, that there was a skepticism to my Dad's voice when I talked with him on the phone twenty minutes ago.

"From there, we'll trap the Reaper and get the evidence we need. Then we can hand the proof to the FBI."

I scoffed to myself. *Easier said than done.*

"Having second thoughts?"

"No," I muttered. "It's just, how are we supposed to knock this thing out? I came at one with a golf club and it didn't seem to make a dent in it. It threw me like a rag doll."

Trent walked up to me and put a hand on my shoulder. "Don't worry so much. That's why I've got all these traps and weapons. I'm not asking you to fight. That's my job." Trent looked up at the sky. "I've got to warm up the truck. It's almost sundown and we'll need to head out shortly after that."

Trent started his truck and sat in the driver seat. I opened the passenger door and plopped in.

"But what if your weapons don't work on it?"

Trent smirked, then pulled a revolver from his glove box.

"There's no going back from a bullet between the eyes, not for anyone. God knows the bastards deserve it." He set the gun down and gripped the steering wheel tight, his knuckles going white. "Is that everything?"

"Just one more thing before we go. What about the exposure we need?"

Trent scrounged a camcorder out of a small black bag and handed it to me. "All you have to do is record on this. Once we get enough footage, we can head to the FBI after knocking it out."

"But--"

"Enough of your concerns, Greg," Trent snapped, lighting up a cigarette. "Either you're in or you're out. You choose." He stared at me intently.

I sighed and shut the passenger door. "Let's go."

CHAPTER 7

Trent and I rode towards the abandoned building in silence, only speaking when I needed to point out a turn or that we had lost our way. There was an angry, determined expression on his face that I both admired and feared. He'd obviously thought about this moment for quite some time, and while I was excited to expose the truth to the masses, I wondered just how far Trent would go for the proof we needed. I mean, we were breaking and entering for Christ's sake.

If we got caught, the jig would be up. All the parents in town would know we knew everything, and there was no telling what they would do to us then. Would they lock us up? Send us away? Sacrifice us to the Reapers?

"Is this it?" Trent asked, shaking me out of my thoughts.

"Um yeah, pull into this empty parking area right here," I gestured to our right.

"Actually, I'm going to pull ahead a bit. It'll make it look less likely that we're here to break into the building."

We parked by the curb ahead of the building and got out. I glanced around. The entire street was deserted. Trent threw some items from the truck bed into a small knapsack, keeping a crowbar in hand. He threw me a flashlight.

"You're the eyes," he said.

We approached the building and tried the metal front door, but it was locked tight.

"Can you bust it open?" I asked.

Trent eyed the frame and lock and frowned. "No, I don't think so. Too sturdy. Let's look around the side."

We turned around the corner to our right and went down the side. As we went, I noticed row upon row of thin, stained glass windows. We continued along until we were out of the moonlight and covered in shadows.

"Stay here," Trent said, pointing further down at what appeared to be a side entrance.

I nodded, turning on my flashlight and going over to the nearest window. I stood on my tiptoes so I could get a glance inside. Through the stained glass, I could make out the shapes of a dozen rows of pews, brightened by the moonlight. This must've been the room that the double doors led to the first time I'd been here.

I heard Trent curse, and he stormed back over. "That door's too strong. We'll have to break one of these windows and have you sneak in. Do you remember this area from your first time here?"

"Uh, yeah, we should be fine," I lied. I felt bad, but how else were we going to get in?

Trent opened up his knapsack and wrapped several layers of thick cloth around a fist. "Stand back," he warned.

He did a test rap against the glass, then the next thing I knew the glass splintered and shattered, tinkling where it fell inside and outside on the pavement. Trent widened the gap enough so I could climb through and put the cloth back in his knapsack.

"You ready?" he asked.

I glanced at the broken window hesitantly. "As I'll ever be."

"Just avoid the glass as much as you can."

Trent made a foothold from his hands and I launched myself up, gripping the outer wall to keep myself steady as I wedged my way inside. I hopped from the ledge and landed with a crunch from the glass beneath me, nearly slipping before I caught my balance.

"Everything okay?" Trent whispered.

"Yeah, I'll go find the side door," I murmured back.

I shined my flashlight around the room once more as I stalked past the rows of dark wooden pews. Tall pillars rose on the outer edges of the worship area, supporting what looked like second floor seating. Up ahead was an alter space with a podium, but it was strangely lacking any crosses or religious icons I knew places like this usually had.

I shivered. It was cold in here, and something about the empty quiet scared me. I skittered to the side door as fast as I could and let Trent in.

"Where to?" he asked.

"This way," I said, pointing back the way I'd come.

We approached the double doors, my stomach in knots. If anyone was lingering around here, they'd catch us pretty easily. I prayed no one was on the other side of those doors.

Trent tried the handle and the door opened. There was nothing but an empty hall ahead of us.

I exhaled in relief.

"I'll check it out first just to be safe," Trent said. "Give me your flashlight."

Trent disappeared into the darkness. I waited for what seemed like an eternity in the cold worship area next to the doors when Trent's head suddenly popped into the room. "All clear."

I jumped. "Christ, you scared the crap outta me!"

Trent shrugged and gave me a pat on the shoulder. "Sorry, man. You'll have to show me the way," he said, handing me the flashlight.

I edged forward, doubt knotting my stomach. *Every-thing's okay. Trent checked out the hallway and no one's here.* Then why did I have such a bad feeling about all of this?

I swallowed my fear, then stepped into the hall with Trent behind me. I shined my light in every direction, casting strange shadows and shapes on the barely furnished walls. We turned the corner into the main hall.

"Which room is it?" Trent asked.

"The one at the far end, straight ahead." I shined my light on the door, and we approached quickly. I tried the door–locked, of course. "How are we going to get into this one?"

Trent eyed the door and frame and grinned. "This one I can break into. Step back and aim your light on the lock, okay?"

"Alright."

I kept my light fixed on the door, catty-cornered as Trent

tried to wedge the edge of the crowbar into the frame just around where the lock was. He jiggled the crowbar this way and that, and slowly it gained purchase inside the door. Satisfied, he gave the bar a swift yank to the right, and the door opened inward with a shower of tiny splinters. I flinched at the cracking sound.

"Let's find the lantern, shall we?" Trent said with a grin.

I was tempted to ask Trent where he'd learned how to pry doors open like that, but instead focused on helping him. The sooner we found the candle, the sooner we'd get out of this hellhole. Lucky for us, the priest had hidden the lantern inside a file cabinet and we found it in just a couple minutes. Trent inspected the candle and I walked out of the room, eager to leave.

A sudden light caught my attention and I turned, wincing as a bright light blinded me.

"Hey, what are you doing in here?" A man shouted.

My heart pounded in my ears. They found us! What would we do? Surely Trent heard the man. The light bobbed closer and closer, and I shielded my eyes, backing up until I hit the wall behind me.

"I said, what are you doing here?"

To my left, Trent suddenly leaped out of the room. The crowbar cracked against the man's body, and he cried out, falling to the floor. No longer blind, I flashed my light in front of me. Trent hovered over the man. He struck him several more times. The man was out cold, and Trent poised to strike again.

"Stop!" I shouted. Trent hesitated, then looked dangerously at the man again. "He's unconscious, isn't that enough?"

Trent glared at me, but gave in and set his crowbar down. He slid his knapsack off and scrounged through it.

"What are you doing? Shouldn't we get out of here?"

"And let this douchebag come find us when he wakes up?" Trent scoffed. "Yeah, no thanks."

Trent pulled some short cords of rope out. "Come on, help me drag this guy into the office."

We left the man tied up in the office with his wrists and ankles behind him. I lingered for a moment, my shoulders slumped. What we were doing felt wrong, but we couldn't let this guy expose us, not when we were so close to the end of our mission. I shined my flashlight back down the hallway. "Back the way we came?"

"No," Trent said. "Who knows if that guy radioed in that someone was in the building. Let's go out the front. Quicker that way."

We ran down the hall to the front door and stopped.

"You ready for the last step?" Trent asked.

I stared down at my feet. That same knotting in my stomach came back, and this time I knew why. After this, we'd be staring death in the face for the second time. I was terrified. As far as I knew, we were the first to ever attempt this. We had a plan, sure, but what if it fell through? Would we die down in my basement?

I pushed my fear back into the corner of my mind. Immy didn't let fear overtake her, and neither would I. "Yeah, my house. Let's go."

I stepped forward to unlock the door when a deafening series of sharp buzzes and whoops thundered around us.

"What the hell?" Trent cried. "That bastard must've called about us!" He looked down the hall back towards the office and clenched his fist around his crowbar, but I grabbed his arm.

"We don't have time. We gotta move!"

Trent growled and slammed the front door open. I ran after him to his pickup truck and we raced away. I glanced behind us through the windshield, wondering how much longer we had before the Order and their army of parents came to hunt us down.

———

Trent's pickup squealed and swerved down mostly vacant city streets as I gripped the grab handle for dear life. The first dozen blocks I thought he was desperate to escape because he was worried we were being followed, but I couldn't see anyone behind us, and we had started to drift off course. I looked to him, confused, and he gave an angry growl that filled the small enclosed space.

"Damn it, they knew! Of course they knew!"

I glared at him. "Would you slow down, already? If you keep driving like this you're going to kill us!"

The pickup veered violently, missing a parked car by inches. He slapped the dashboard with a hand and laughed to himself.

Something about his outburst knocked something loose

within me, and I undid my seat belt and lunged at the steering wheel for control. "God damn it, I said stop!"

For a moment we continued to swerve, then Trent hit the brake hard. I smacked against the dashboard, my shoulders and back flaring with pain.

I grumbled as I collected myself. "What the hell is wrong with you? Have you gone crazy?"

Trent put his head to his hands on the steering wheel. "They knew we'd come for the candle. They freaking knew! What makes you think we'll pull this thing off?"

I pried Trent's fingers off the steering wheel and pulled him to face me. "You can't let your emotions get the best of you. Not when we're this close. Danny and Imogen deserve justice, and we're going to give it to them."

Trent looked at me with red, watery eyes. "I'm sorry. I'm just so freaking mad. At the parents, at those fucking Reapers, at this whole screwed up situation." He looked out his window briefly. "I shouldn't have left that guy in one piece."

"Hey, you spared that guy's life back there. If you ask me, that takes guts, regardless of what happened after."

Trent nodded and gave a sad smile as his expression lightened.

"We're in this crappy situation together, and we're going to see it through. But you have to calm down. The alarm only went off a few minutes ago. It's going to take the parents time to get to that building, let alone find the guy we tied up. And even then, do you think he recognized us? I doubt it."

Trent smiled, this time more strongly. "Yeah, you're right.

Sorry I lost control back there. I'll drive more carefully now. Lead the way to your place?"

I nodded and pointed him onward, glad his eyes were on the road instead of me. Truth be told, I didn't doubt the guy recognized us, not one bit. I'd seen a flash of recognition when Trent first assaulted him, right before his expression morphed into pain and terror. But what Trent needed was a voice of reason, and I guess that was me, odd enough as it was.

When we turned onto my street minutes later, my spine shivered. The street was almost completely empty of cars, which was weird for my street on any day. We pulled into my driveway and Trent cut the engine, but I hesitated.

"Something wrong?" Trent asked.

I thought it over. Something was definitely off. Where were all the parents' cars? Were they driving around town looking for us, or did they already know we were coming and vacated for some reason? I shook my head. Either way, it was too late to turn back now. We had to do this for Danny, for Imogen. For all of the lost kids. "No, it's nothing. Let's head inside."

CHAPTER 8

I hung over the backside of the living room couch, peeping out through the front window from behind the curtains in complete darkness. *Still clear.*

After we went inside, made sure no one was home, and got all of Trent's tools and traps in the basement, he told me to go upstairs to keep a lookout so he could set everything up. It had been nearly twenty minutes, and left to my own devices I was really starting to get antsy.

By now the Order's parents would've gotten back to their secret building and rescued the man Trent and I had tied up. He definitely knew Trent and saw me, but would that lead them back here? While there weren't any direct ties between me and my new friend and I'd never seen the man before, my family was the last to have a kid go missing. It wouldn't take much to connect the dots, and there was no telling how much time we had left now. Any minute and it could all be over.

"Greg, come down here!" Trent called.

I jogged over to the basement landing and started down the steps. About halfway, I stopped dead in my tracks. Numerous traps littered the basement: bear traps lay on the floor, rope nets were sprawled out in every direction, and an unused trip wire sat on a nearby table next to a shotgun. Trent's hands were currently entangled in a large net of thick white rope.

Something in here was bound to kill or at least maim the Reaper that took my little sister away, but I was hoping Trent would've been ready by now.

Trent looked up from the jumble of rope in his hands. "Did you see anything?"

"No, not yet. Why'd you call me down here? You don't look anywhere near ready."

He frowned. "Yeah, it's taking me longer than I thought. This basement is sturdy, but its not necessarily the best for laying traps. Do you have anything that would camouflage this rope?"

I glanced around. "Yeah, you could use some of the covers for the old furniture around here." I turned to leave.

"Hey, is everything okay?"

I spun around and folded my arms. "What do you mean?"

"You seem upset."

I scoffed. "Hopeless describes it better." I tried to hold back the frustration and disappointment I felt, but it came pouring out. "Do you really think a few measly traps are going to kill the monster? The Reaper took my sister so fast I could hardly react, and even when I did, it could've killed me. What makes you think any of this is going to work?"

Trent grimaced and set the rope down. "Listen, I totally understand your skepticism. To be honest, half of these traps probably won't work on it. But there's a chance, and all I can do is try. If you want, I can do this alone. You can keep watch upstairs while I take this thing out. But Gregory, I am going to do this, and nothing is going to stop me except that freaking beast itself."

The fight in me gave out. Trent was right. We'd come so far. As much as I wanted to run, I actually cared about Trent's well-being. I didn't want him to sacrifice himself only to fail.

Somewhere deep down, I knew that if Trent faced the monster alone, he would die. I couldn't let him do that. I had to help him. Otherwise, how could I live with myself? I hadn't really been living since Immy was taken from me, just like he hadn't since he lost Danny. I clenched my fists. If I was going to die tonight, I was taking that Reaper with me. "I want to fight."

Trent's eyes widened. "You, but I thoug--"

"I'm not going to let you fight that monster on your own. This isn't just your fight, it's mine too. Give me a weapon."

Trent smiled and rummaged through the miscellaneous items littering the floor. He came up with an item in each hand. "Butcher knife or handaxe?"

I walked up to him and took the butcher knife. "Thanks. We'll end this together. I'm gonna go keep an eye upstairs. You finish setting up here and let me know when you're ready." I turned to leave.

"Alright buddy, and hey."

I spun back around.

"Thanks, for everything."

I grinned. "Think nothing of it."

I hopped up the stairs, fear and excitement rushing over me. We were going to do this. We could show the world what was happening here. People would understand us, find a way so that no one else's sister or brother would have to die in vain. I sat down on the living room couch and drew back the curtain.

My heart skipped a beat. In the moonlight, I could make out four tall figures approaching my driveway from across the street. The parents were coming for us. As they neared, I could hear some of them talking softly thanks to the silence of the street.

"See, that Duffy kid's pickup is here, just like Roy said," one of them said.

"Okay, I'm sorry for doubting you," a familiar voice apologized. "I just ... I just didn't want to believe that my Gregory would do this."

My pulse thundered in my ears. *Mom?*

"Hey, everything's fine," another parent said. "We just need to get in there and stop those boys."

I jumped off the couch and ran to the dining room as fast as my feet would carry me. I shouldn't have wasted time listening to them! I had to stall them, even if just a little. I grabbed the nearest chair and hobbled back to the front door, propping it underneath the knob and shifting it until it held tight.

I sprinted back to the basement landing, not bothering

to watch my volume anymore. "Trent, light the candle! They're here!"

As I reached the door, I ripped the padlock off the outside. I went inside and closed the door behind me, fumbling with the lock as my fingers trembled. We were completely, utterly screwed.

CHAPTER 9

I barrelled down the stairs, my stomach dropping as soon as I saw the condition of the basement. The traps weren't ready, and Trent was pacing back and forth, gripping his rusty brown hair.

"Shit, shit, shit! What're we supposed to do now?" he asked me.

I found it hard to answer him. Our mission was pretty much suicide now. I mean, sure, we had weapons, but without any traps ready we had no plan of attack. My nose scrunched as I passed through the stream of foul smoke from the candle at the foot of the stairs.

"I don't know, but we have to pull it together. That candle works fast, and the parents will be coming after us once they unblock the door."

"Thanks for the reminder, captain obvious," Trent grunted.

I swallowed my annoyance at his attitude and glanced

over the traps in front of me. "Which traps take the least amount of time to set up?"

Trent scanned the messy floor and sighed. "The bear traps, I guess."

"Alright, do that. But watch out for the door. If it appears, holler. I'll move the camcorder somewhere safe. What's our plan?"

"I don't know, alright?" Trent stopped what he was doing for a moment, then breathed heavily. "If we can place the bear traps around the door when it appears, that should do some serious damage. Then I can shoot the bastard."

"What if that doesn't work?"

"Then it's either stabbing the thing to death or lighting it on fire." Trent nodded to the table by the landing to his left. On top was a bottle of lighter fluid.

I groaned internally. So it was either get stab-happy or burn my house to the ground. What great options. I glanced at the butcher knife in my hand. *Let's hope plan A works out.* The last thing I wanted to do was fight a Reaper in close range given last time's outcome.

A loud crash upstairs made Trent and I jump. Heavy footsteps echoed down to us, and my mother's voice rang through like a bell as she pounded on the basement door.

"Gregory?" she called. "Gregory, please talk to me."

I gawked at Trent and he waved me off. "Deal with it. Just don't open the door."

I walked over to the base of the stairs and made my way up, stopping just a few feet from the top.

"Gregory, I want you to open this door right now," she said in a commanding tone.

"You know I can't do that, not after what happened to Immy."

"Honey, you don't understand. We had to do it. Please, just let me in and we can talk this all over before anyone gets hurt."

"Oh, so you just *had* to sacrifice her? Christ, Mom! You took a freaking paycheck to get rid of her. What else is there to explain? This is why we have to expose the Reapers. It's time we fought back, time we end this."

Trent cried out, "Greg, get your ass down here!"

My mom pounded desperately on the door. "Gregory, no! You don't know what you're doing!"

My mother's shrieks faded as I reached the basement floor. Nothing was going to stop me; there was no turning back from this. I set the camcorder under the table to the left of the landing. Trent came up to me, armed with his rifle and several weapons dangling from a makeshift strap around his waist.

"I put the bear traps close to the door. You let me blast that fucker first, got it? Once I injure it enough we'll both go to town on it and finish this. Okay?"

I gulped. "Uh, yeah." I gripped my butcher knife harder, but my palms were getting sweaty so I wiped them on my pants.

I hesitantly looked at the strange door that had yet again appeared in the middle of my basement. It seemed the same as before. The same rickety gray vertical planks, the same black puffs of smoke curling from underneath, the same strange, eerie yellow-- *Oh God.*

"Trent, it's coming!" I whispered frantically.

He gripped my shoulder. "This is it. Get to the right and take cover. I'll attack it from here."

I darted past the strange door, not daring to look at it, and hid behind a large covered couch. For several moments, all was silent in the basement. I could even hear my own unsteady breathing.

I poked my head out for a glance when the strange door swung open with great force. It slammed against the concrete wall as a tall, towering form ducked its head under the frame. It straightened and nearly touched the ceiling.

I tried to analyze the monster under its dark, tattered robes, but couldn't tell if it was the same one that took Immy or not. Besides, I'd only seen one. Maybe they all looked the same. Regardless, my heart thundered in my chest like an overpowered piston. The monster stood in place, almost seeming uncertain of its surroundings. I guessed it was hoping for an easy kill. *Think again, asshole.*

With a snap of its head, the monster glared in my direction. I darted beneath my cover, willing myself not to breathe. *Crap! What if it comes for me first?* Our whole plan would be ruined.

"Hey, fuckface!" Trent called.

I peered over the covered arm of the sofa. The Reaper was now focused on Trent, who was standing ten feet away from it with his shotgun poised. A foot or two ahead of the Reaper were the first of the bear traps.

"Smile for the camera," Trent sneered.

With a deep, monstrous growl, the Reaper lunged towards Trent only to stop dead in its tracks when one of the bear traps snapped closed with a crunching, metallic clang.

The ear-wrenching shriek of pain that came from the monster nearly made me drop my knife. I covered my ears with a smile. *So far so good.*

However, my happiness was short lived. The Reaper continued to shriek and howl, and its body began to flail violently, like dead tree branches in a hurricane. A strange kind of static seemed to fill the air, and the hairs on my body stood on end. Without warning, the other nearby bear traps lifted in the air and launched of their own accord, followed by the one that had clamped onto its foot. I ducked my head, and they crashed against the far walls, clanging to the ground.

Luckily, none of them had been close enough to hit Trent or me, but my whole body quaked. What the hell was that? Could the Reaper move things with its mind? Jesus Christ, we had to kill this thing before it tried that again. I peeked my head out for another look.

Trent gawked at the monster. His face was pale, and I couldn't blame him. He hesitated for just a moment before aiming his gun, but it was a moment the monster already had on him. Even with its limp, the Reaper slammed into him, sending him flying back. He hit the wall hard and fell to the ground, his shotgun clattering next to him. He didn't move.

Shit, shit, shit. What was I supposed to do now? The monster had a crippled leg, but obviously it could still throw us around like rag dolls.

The monster limped rather casually towards Trent, its long spindly fingers reaching out towards him. My little sister's face flashed in my mind.

I ran from my cover after the monster, rage coursing through my veins. I grabbed the butcher knife with both hands and leaped into the air. My knife plunged into the monster's back almost effortlessly, and my weight sank the blade in even further as I dangled in the air.

The deafening bellow that came from the Reaper was excruciating, but I held firm as I hung above the ground, my blade dragging deeper. The monster spun around so fast I was flung into a column of cardboard boxes, which fell all around me, but my eyes were still focused on the beast. A gooey, black ooze dripped to the floor from where I'd stabbed it. The Reaper screeched and clutched awkwardly at the knife protruding from its back, but its spidery fingers couldn't grip it.

Then slowly, the knife began to inch out of its back. I gaped at the spectacle before me. The Reaper really *could* move things with its mind. What exactly *was* this thing? Just before the knife pulled out fully, the blade caught on the Reaper's robe.

In one swift supernatural motion, the knife went flying to a corner of the basement. The large hole it ripped in the robes stretched and tore, unraveling and sliding off inch by inch until it fell to the floor.

My breathing stopped as I took in the monster's naked appearance. The Reaper's gaunt, bony body was covered in huge, ripe boils. The flesh around them was so wrinkled I wondered how ancient this thing was. Its body gave off a rotten, sickening odor that made me cover my nose, even from ten feet away. I fought the vomit that threatened to come up.

I wanted to scream, I wanted to run. I wanted to burst through the basement window and let the shards bite into me. Anything to get me away from this god-awful freak.

The Reaper's piercing yellow eyes sized me up and it gave a hideous growl, exposing several rows of jagged, broken teeth. In a split second, I was up and sprinting down the other side of the basement. As I ran, I pulled down anything I could get my hands on to slow the bastard down. A chair here, a table there, the old birdcage I'd mistaken for Immy a month ago. As I neared the far end of the basement, a loud clatter erupted and I spun around.

The Reaper was hunched over the birdcage, which was now half-destroyed and resembled a broken ribcage. A tingle of warmth spread through my chest. Its injuries were slowing it down, at least for now. I probably wouldn't get another chance like this. I slipped around a tower of boxes to my left and allowed myself a deep breath.

Trent had said we had two options, stabbing it to death and ... yes, burning it! But the lighter fluid he'd pointed out to me was on the other side of the basement. That meant getting past the Reaper in one piece.

I glanced around the stack of boxes. The Reaper was still resting against the birdcage, but its labored breathing had steadied a bit. I didn't have much longer before it would come after me again.

I darted back out of sight. A number of chairs, couches, and other bulky items lined the way back towards Trent. If I could crawl under them, maybe I could get back to the lighter fluid and avoid the monster.

I glanced back the way I'd come where the monster was

recovering. I gasped. The Reaper was gone, only the shattered remains of the old birdcage left behind. I stepped back. *Where did it--*

A flurry of inhumanely long fingers raked at me as the beast darted from the shadows. I stumbled on my own feet and landed on my butt, somehow avoiding the beast's attack.

I half scrambled, half crawled back towards my escape, praying the Reaper wouldn't get to me before I hit cover. By some stroke of luck, I made it under a large couch. I shuffled my way underneath, scrambling for the next cover. As soon as my feet cleared, I heard a splintering crash right behind me. Splinters of wood and fabric flew around as the couch broke into pieces with a wrathful shriek from the monster.

My pulse pounded in my ears. He was right behind me. I increased my pace as much as I could. With the clearing of each cover, my protection would go flying against the wall and ceiling with another otherworldly cry, each time closer than before. I thought for sure the Reaper would get me, but once I cleared the last of my cover, a large elevated sectional, I knew I was safe for at least the next few seconds. The item was large enough that it would be hard for anyone to move–including the beast, I hoped.

Once clear of the sectional I darted ahead, not looking back. Trent was still where he'd fallen, the shotgun in front of him. He was conscious, but looked extremely dazed. I dove for the lighter fluid and spun back around. The Reaper turned the corner and came at me with a wail.

I squirted the lighter fluid right at its face. The Reaper screamed and fell back, rubbing at its eyes with the corner of its hand. I continued spraying the fluid over it. This was it. But wait, I needed a lighter. Shit!

"Trent, give me your lighter! Trent, come on!"

I turned back briefly, and he fumbled with his pocket before handing me his zippo. By the time I looked back towards the monster, it was about to pounce. I clicked the flame on and tossed it.

The Reaper's body erupted in flames. It cried out in pain and ran off, banging against the walls and flailing its long, spindly hands. I heard a loud crash then, but ignored it. Trent and I had to get out of here before the Reaper set the entire basement on fire.

"Trent, we've got to go, come on."

I wrapped my arms around him and lifted with a grunt. He groaned, pushing against the wall for support with his uninjured hand.

"I think my arm is broken," he muttered into my ear.

"It doesn't matter. We've gotta get up those stairs." I half-dragged Trent over to the stairs, everything drowned out by the terrible screams of the Reaper and my heartbeat throbbing in my head.

I guided him to the railing, then released him and pushed from behind. Looking up, I saw what the loud crash had been. My mom stood at the top of the stairs. She smiled at me before her face morphed into terror.

"Gregory, behind you!"

I spun back around. The Reaper was nearly on me, its yellow eyes glaring through the flames that licked its skin. I freaked, and in my haste to climb away from it, my feet tangled on themselves. I fell with a thud. I tried to crabwalk up, but it was right on me. It was too late.

The Reaper raised a long, flaming hand to strike, and then another loud bang came from behind me. A small crater appeared right between the monster's eyes, and black ooze poured out of the wound in a steady river. Its eyes were vacant as it wavered back and fell to the concrete, unmoving.

I glanced back, shocked. My mom had a revolver in her hand, still fixated on the collapsed monster. "Mom?"

Mom lowered her weapon and smiled sadly. "Are you alright?"

"I'm fine," I growled, remembering her part in all this.

She frowned and looked up the stairs with a wave. "All clear down here."

Two men came barrelling down the stairs, one holding a fire extinguisher. They passed my mom and gathered around the monster hesitantly. One pulled out a gun and shot it several more times in the head. The other doused the creature and nearby items that had caught fire.

I felt sick to my stomach, but tried to contain myself. I glanced around, puzzled. "Where's Trent?"

"Your dad is upstairs bandaging him up and explaining what's happening."

"What do you mean? We already know what the adults in town have been doing, what *you've* been doing."

Mom sat down on the stair next to me. She tried to put a hand on my shoulder, but I flinched. "I guess I deserve that based on what you already know, but it's not what you think."

"Oh yeah? I know you *sacrificed* Immy to those freaking monsters. You took money after letting the Reaper kill her."

"You're right about the money. I can't even begin to tell you how sorry I am for that. But Gregory, this is the way of the world. The Order has had this system in place for decades. Fighting them on this ..." She looked away. "It wasn't an option. But when I saw that beast ... I couldn't just let it take you too. And now I fear we've opened Pandora's box."

"What do you mean?"

Mom opened her mouth to answer, but a blood-curdling scream sounded from far away. "No," she whimpered, her voice shaky. She got to her feet and charged up the stairs, and I followed her.

When we got upstairs, Dad was standing with Trent behind the living room curtains peeking outside.

"George, how bad is it?" Mom asked.

Dad turned around and simply shook his head. Mom's face lost all color, and she bolted to the front door, yanking it open and running outside.

"Patricia!" Dad yelled after her.

I followed after Mom, darting down the driveway to catch up with her. The sight before me brought tears to my eyes. The street was in complete chaos. Numerous bodies littered the lawns of nearby houses, some moving slowly, some not at all.

Across the street, a woman was fighting off another Reaper with a long knife, but she was losing the battle. She saw us, and waved frantically. "Help me!"

The Reaper knocked the knife from her hands and put

its long spindly fingers around her head. Our neighbor's face loosened, then deadened as her face drained to a dead gray. The Reaper released its grip on her and she fell to the ground like a rock.

Mom said something, but I couldn't hear her. All of this, it was happening because of Trent and I. We thought we knew everything, but ... we had started a war.

Mom grabbed my shoulders and gave them a shake. "Gregory, inside. *Now.*"

The Reaper across the street saw us and headed our way.

Warm tears ran down my cheeks as we withdrew inside. "What have we done?"

EPILOGUE

If you are reading this now, I am either dead or have fled elsewhere. It has been five days, five days of hell since the Reapers came for us. In their first attack, we lost more people than I can count. Dad lost his life protecting Trent, Mom, and I. I'm still coming to grips with that.

After two days we had to leave the house. The three of us simply couldn't protect it anymore and by then the electricity had gone out. Ironically enough, we shacked up with the surviving adults, FBI agents, and children at the abandoned building that the Order had used.

We've been able to hold the Reapers off, but their numbers are increasing. It's clear that our town is no longer safe. We prepare to leave this god-forsaken place at dawn to find somewhere secure. I want to be optimistic, but whenever I ask the adults how far spread the Reapers are, they simply won't answer me. I've decided to keep holding on to hope. It's all I've got at this point.

No doubt by now you know the truth. You're probably fighting those bastards off yourself. But if you aren't, if by some stroke of luck you aren't under attack, you still have a chance out there. Whatever you do, listen to your parents. If they light strange, white candles, let them burn. But if you see a strange door appear out of nowhere, run. Run for your life.

THE END

ACKNOWLEDGMENTS

I couldn't have written this story without the help of my Scribophile tribe: Emerald, Marvin, Randy, Sarah, and Victoria.

A very heartfelt thanks goes out to Emerald, who helped guide me through the entire process. I couldn't have done this without you.

Last but not least, I would like to thank all of my alpha and beta readers. You've helped me more than you could ever know.

ABOUT THE AUTHOR

Jonathan Pongratz is a writer and author of captivating horror, urban fantasy, and paranormal stories. When he's not writing, he's busy being a bookworm, video game junkie, and karaoke vocalist. A former resident of Dallas, he currently resides in Kansas City with his halloween cat Ajax. By day he works magic in finance, by night he creates dark and mesmerizing worlds.

Visit his blog at:
www.Jonathanpongratz.tumblr.com
Visit his website at:
www.jonathanpongratz.com

JONATHAN PONGRATZ

www.ingramcontent.com/pod-product-compliance
Lightning Source LLC
Chambersburg PA
CBHW030755110726
47900CB00008B/2608